Terry and Freddie

Mark Albini

Published in the United States of America

ISBN 978-1-962569-49-1 (SC)
ISBN 978-1-962730-97-6 (HC)

Mark Albini Publishing
155 weeping Willow Dr.,
Myrtle Beach South Carolina 29579
rhyminganimaladventures@yahoo.com.

Order Information and Rights Permission:

Quantity sales. Special discounts might be available on quantity purchases by corporations, associations, and others. For details, contact the publisher at the address above.

For Book Rights Adaptation and other Rights Permission.
Call us at toll-free 1-888-945-8513 or send us an email at
admin@stellarliterary.com.

Acknowledgements

A Special Thank You to my wife, Sharyn Albini, who had to listen to all the writes and rewrites over the years.

Dedicated to my parents, Louis Alfred Albini and Katherine Jeannine Albini.

Inspired by my love for animals, my love for America, my father Louis Albini, and Clement C. Moore.

Honoring my Christian Faith, my good friends and a few people from the past who were very special to me. I've used their names as the names of my characters in the Rescue Ranch Series. I had so many friends with the name Bob I had to use the name Bobo to cover them all. They became the voice of wisdom on the farm and it was a fun way to keep my friends around me. This way we could all live forever in the stories. I won't get them all in but I'm going to try.

The Creation of Rescue Ranch

It all began the day Grandpa Eddie purchased an old farmhouse that sat on a large parcel of land. The farmhouse was a few hundred miles from an old country zoo he used to visit as a boy. The zoo was closing after its caretaker had passed away but a family member stayed on to run the zoo until she could find a home for the animals. The Giraffes were chosen to be the first to go. Grandpa Eddie agreed to take the Giraffe family and drove up to the old farmhouse just in time to see the Giraffes arrive. They were dropped off in a field that backed up to an old red barn across the street from the house. Jimmy was excited to have a new home but surprised to find out he had to get up early. Tomorrow was a school day. On his way there he passed a shed with a beautiful white horse named Howie. Howie became Jimmy's best friend and on most days Jimmy would stop by in the morning and they would walk to school together. Some of the buildings they passed along the way had been rundown for years and it was obvious there was a lot to do on this old farm. Grandpa Eddie woke up early everyday of his life and went right to work. He needed to make room for some of the animals he was hoping to rescue. He planted some crops, cleaned out the barn and went looking for a hog to put in the sty. It didn't take long before it started to feel like home. He decided to call it The Rescue Ranch.

INTRODUCTION

The Rescue Ranch is a peaceful place where
animals live in wide open space.
They're fed everyday and have plenty to eat.
Life on this farm is really quite sweet.
It's a place for animals to come and stay and
meet new friends and have fun each day.
The animals are friendly and very sincere and
most have retired from a long career.
Except for those who were born on the farm and
a few in the woods that have caused alarm
If they live in the woods or somewhere on the farm
they all contribute to its countryside charm.
So welcome to the Rescue Ranch where
animals receive an olive branch.

Book #1   Jimmy the Giraffe
Book #2   Ricky the Rabbit
and Bobo the Mouse
Book #3   Terry the Turtle
and Freddie the Fish
Book #4   Sammy the
Snake – Coming Soon

RESCUE
RANCH

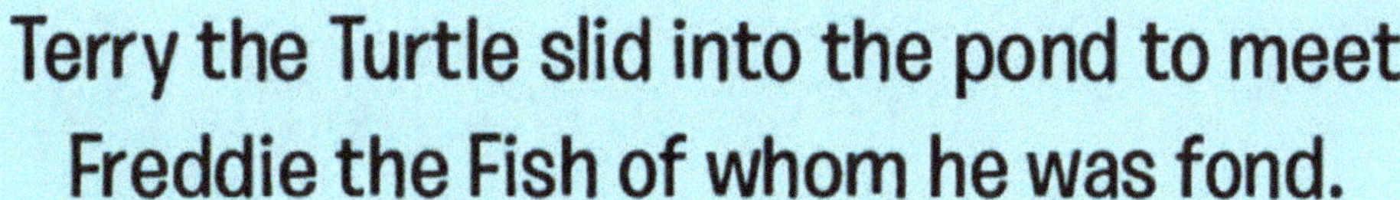

Terry the Turtle slid into the pond to meet
Freddie the Fish of whom he was fond.

It was 12 o'clock noon that time of the day, when
Terry and Freddie would sneak off to play.
Freddie the Fish had school until three but he
hoped to leave early and let no one see.

Terry the Turtle took a nap in his bed and let
visions of racing dance around in his head.
While Terry and Freddie had plans for a race,
Freddie thought Terry could never keep pace.

Freddie was fast. Why, he'd never been beat.
He won every race and he loved to compete.
He was so fast that he learned how to fly.
He'd turn his fins down and soar up to the sky.
And Terry the Turtle was a little too slow.
He raced underwater and liked staying below.

Then Freddie the Fish broke an old rule when he fled from the rocks and played hooky from school.

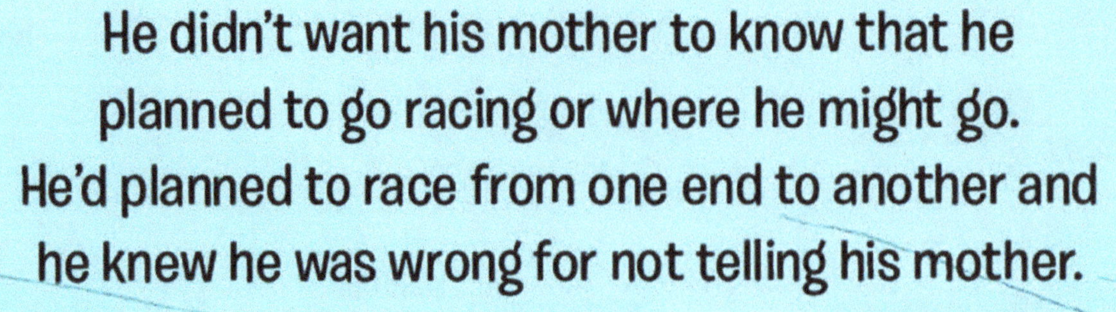

He didn't want his mother to know that he
planned to go racing or where he might go.
He'd planned to race from one end to another and
he knew he was wrong for not telling his mother.

He began to feel guilty for leaving his class as he swam
from the rocks and very fast through the grass.

Some shadows were cast at the edge of the bank
as a giraffe and a horse knelt down and drank.
It was Jimmy the Giraffe and his very good pal,
Howie the Horse, down from the corral.

Bobo the Mouse hid under the hay and hitched
a free ride to watch Freddie that day.
They came to the pond to see the big race and
watch Terry the Turtle try to keep pace.

Freddie the Fish was sure that he'd win and for
most of the day his mouth had a grin.

Until he saw Terry with a smile on his face and that cast some doubt as they lined up to race.
START
11

Then Terry got scared when he saw something black.
It was Sammy the Snake about to attack.

12

Terry came up for air yelling "go Freddie go,
fly up to the sky and then dive down below."

13

So Freddie flew up and out of the pond.
It was almost as if he had his own magic wand.
He dove in the water and hid near the bank.
He was safe for the moment and had Terry to thank.

14

Jimmy and Howie jumped to their feet cheering
for Freddie from their ring side seat.
Bobo climbed from the hay with a smile on his
face hoping to see Freddie win the big race.

But Sammy the Snake kept lurking around and
snuck up behind Freddie without even a sound.

Then Terry the Turtle got a plan up his sleeve.
"If I bite Sammy's tail maybe then he would leave".

So Terry the Turtle dove down real deep and
snuck up on Sammy without making a peep.

18

He opened his mouth and bit Sammy's tail
and it hurt so bad that it turned Sammy pale.

Sammy swam from the pond and into the grass while
Freddie was wishing he'd just stayed in his class.
Bobo the Mouse dove under the hay when he
saw that Sammy was heading his way.

20

Then Jimmy and Howie decided to leave
with a flying fish story no one would believe.
A lesson was learned from this foolish mistake.
Don't ever go swimming near Sammy the Snake.

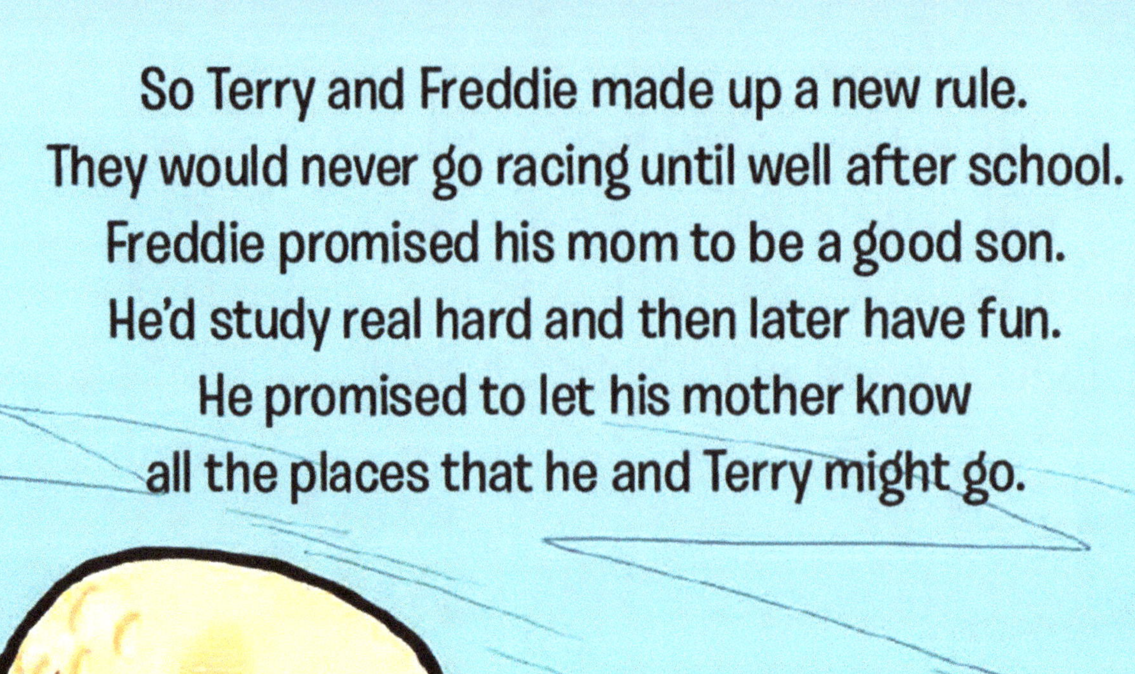

So Terry and Freddie made up a new rule.
They would never go racing until well after school.
Freddie promised his mom to be a good son.
He'd study real hard and then later have fun.
He promised to let his mother know
all the places that he and Terry might go.

The Rescue Ranch Family